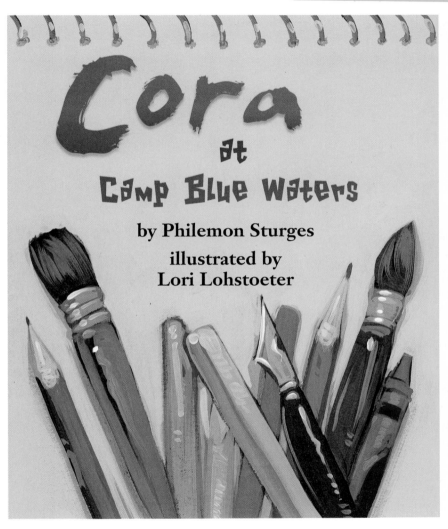

Cora

at
Camp Blue Waters

by Philemon Sturges

illustrated by
Lori Lohstoeter

HOUGHTON MIFFLIN

BOSTON

Cora was an indoor girl, a homebody. Her favorite hobby was drawing. She mostly drew the ideas in her head. "I like to use my imagination," she said.

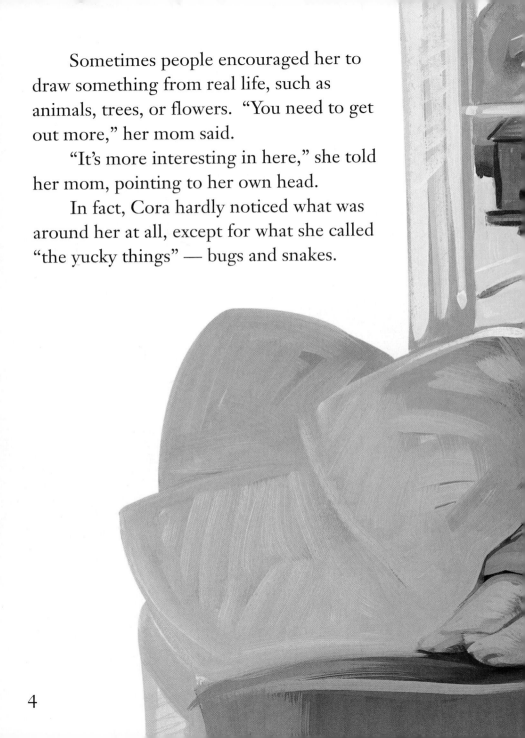

Sometimes people encouraged her to draw something from real life, such as animals, trees, or flowers. "You need to get out more," her mom said.

"It's more interesting in here," she told her mom, pointing to her own head.

In fact, Cora hardly noticed what was around her at all, except for what she called "the yucky things" — bugs and snakes.

So Cora was not excited when her dad said that she'd be going to Camp Blue Waters that summer.

"Why me?" wailed Cora.

"Mom and I think you'd like the great outdoors if you'd give it a chance," said Cora's dad. "Besides, it's only for two weeks. Your pens and paper will be here when you get back."

"Your cousin Teri's going too! She went to Camp Blue Waters last summer, and she loved it," said Cora's mom. "You told me you never get to spend enough time with Teri. Here's your chance."

Cora couldn't fall asleep that night. She kept thinking about what was waiting for her at Camp Blue Waters. (Cora's imagination helped her draw, but it didn't help her sleep.) Ugh, thought Cora. I'm going to spend the next two weeks sweating and itching in the hot sun.

Even the thought of being with Teri didn't help.

Cora didn't sleep well during her first night at Camp Blue Waters, either. Things weren't quite as bad as she thought they'd be, but there *were* flies buzzing near the screen, and there *was* a spider in the shower. Moths flew around the light outside her cabin door. Owls hooted in the trees. Even Teri made noises in her sleep. And Cora just knew there was a bear nearby.

The next morning, it rained. Still, Cora and Teri's camp leader, Anne, took everyone outside for a tour of the camp.

They passed smooth playing fields and softly rolling hills. They saw a still, dark lake with a pale, sandy beach. Then they walked through the deep, green woods.

But all Cora saw was poison ivy, thorns, and sticks that looked like snakes. When she jumped away from one especially snaky stick, she slipped on some wet grass and fell into a muddy puddle.

Cora was nearly in tears when Anne and Teri pulled her up.

Anne said, "Let's get out of the rain for a little while." She led the girls to a large building. Inside was a huge room with a stage at one end and folding chairs at the other.

"This is where we put on plays and concerts," she said. Then she led them to another room.

Anne opened the door and said, "And this is the arts and crafts room." It was filled with big tables and easels. There were boxes of pencils, paints, and scissors. And there were shelves of paper, all kinds of paper.

"And this is the arts and crafts teacher, Bill," said Anne. Bill gave the girls a friendly wink.

Neat, thought Cora. Now if I could just stay in this room for two weeks. . . .

Cora *did* go to the arts and crafts room
every day. But she didn't stay there. Bill often
told everyone to pack up their paper and
pencils and paints and go outside.

"But why?" Cora asked, the first time they went out. "I have plenty of ideas in my own head. I don't need to look at things outside."

But Bill told her, "An artist always uses what's inside, even when she draws outside. Just give it a try! I'll be there to help."

Bill showed Cora how to choose colors that matched nature. He taught her to see shapes and patterns in the leaves, and how to make living things look round on flat paper. He taught her to draw flowers, bugs, fish, and a rabbit she saw on the lawn.

When Cora showed Bill her drawing of two robins in a twisty old apple tree, he called her a "real wildlife artist."

Now when Cora drew outdoors, she wasn't bothered by poison ivy, or thorns, or bugs. She was too busy noticing the blue petals that matched the color of the sky. And when she saw sticks that looked like snakes, she wished they *were* snakes, so she could draw them.

After she got home, Cora kept drawing
outside as much as she could. One snowy day,
as she sat indoors drawing the beautiful ideas
that lived in her head, she noticed that the
outside had come in.